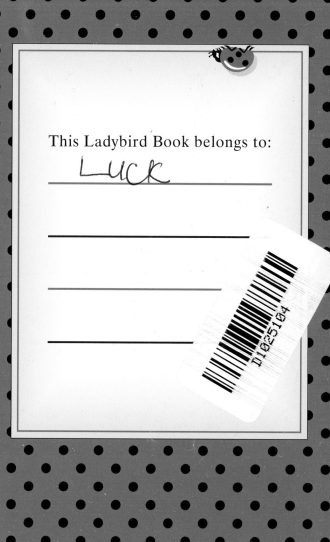

This Ladybird Book belongs to:

LUCK

Let's read together readers and activity books are designed for you and your child to share.

This old man is based on the well-known rhyme, which all children love. The rhyme is given on the left-hand page for the adult to read to the child. On the right-hand page, words from the rhyme are repeated, and new words are added to help your child to join in.

First read the book aloud. Then go through the rhyme again, this time encouraging your child to read the text on the right-hand page. The illustrations give picture cues to the words. Many young children will remember the words rather than be able to read them, but this is an important part of learning to read. Always praise as you go along – keep your reading sessions fun, and stop if your child loses interest.

Ladybird books are widely available, but in case of difficulty may be ordered by post or telephone from:

Ladybird Books – Cash Sales Department
Littlegate Road Paignton Devon TQ3 3BE
Telephone 01803 554761

A catalogue record for this book is available
from the British Library

Published by Ladybird Books Ltd Loughborough Leicestershire UK
Ladybird Books Inc Auburn Maine 04210 USA

Ladybird

This old man

by Karen Bryant-Mole
illustrated by John Blackman

This old man, he played one.
He played knick, knack
On his drum...

I like my drum.

With a knick, knack
Paddy whack
Give a dog a bone...

This old man came
Rolling home.

9

This old man, he played two.
He played knick, knack
On his shoe...

Are these my shoes?

This old man, he played three.
He played knick, knack
On his knee…

1

2

3

These are my knees.

This old man, he played four.
He played knick, knack
On the floor...

1
2
3
4

Look at me!

This old man, he played five.
He played knick, knack
Doing a dive...

I like to swim!

This old man, he played six.
He played knick, knack
With some sticks...

This dog likes sticks.

This old man, he played seven.
He played knick, knack
Up to heaven ...

Up I go!

21

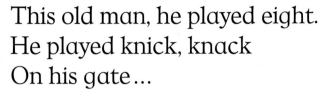

This old man, he played eight.
He played knick, knack
On his gate...

22

1
2
3
4
5
6
7
8

Here is my house.

23

This old man, he played nine.
He played knick, knack
On the line...

I have fun.

This old man, he played ten.
He played knick, knack
All over again.